The Church Tried to Shame Me

Elaine Jenkins

Published by G Miller, 2023.

THE CHURCH TRIED TO SHAME ME

First edition. February 25, 2023.

Copyright © 2023 Elaine Jenkins.

ISBN: 979-8215900796

Written by Elaine Jenkins.

Table of Contents

Synopsis

My friends and family call me Jess, graduated Summa Cum Laude from Spelman College with a BA in Marketing. I'm a senior credit analyst for a small marketing firm. I secured this job after being employed on an internship that I secured my senior year.

When I came to school I didn't intend on the events that happened, but I wouldn't trade it for nothing. Being raised in a very strict spiritual household was tough. My parents had me and my siblings (Josiah and Jaleesa) at every church function up and down the east coast. To their defense love was expressed verbal and physical, with minimal communication. To their fault the truth of the world was not explained nor encouraged to be aware of; they assumed we knew.

So, who goes off to college and loses all her mind? Yes, that would be me Jessica "Jess" Smith. I was on every set, dances, parties, games, and other outside activity that didn't include church. I pledged in my sophomore year. Ms. New Beginning #8, Spring 2016 of Delta Sigma Theta Sorority. All the things I was taught was inside, but it laid dormant; yes, put on the back burner.

I managed to meet a handsome guy, a taller version of Michael B Jordan. I met Jason Miguel St. John. He was a junior studying Political Science at Morehouse when we met. I was not quickly sold on dating him at first, he was very persistent. He was at a campus party for all the Greeks, athletes and who's who was attending that night.

I know I was playing hard to get. Within a short time, me and Jason were a hot item around the schools.

Of course, your path doesn't plan out the way you want them. I thought I would come to school, learn, and then go home and get back into the routine of being the perfect church girl my parents raised. That all fell apart when one steamy night I found myself in a class called Sin Sister Sin 101. Yes, me and Jason were playing house. That led to me having to make a confession to my parents that they were going to be grandparents.

Within less than 10 months of our relationship, Jason had made me a woman. I was no longer a virgin; I was a sexual slave to both our wants and needs. Later that following summer I gave birth to a handsome baby boy that resembled his father. Jayce Michael St. John was born.

I was badly criticized for becoming an out of wedlock mother. That would bring me to explain who my judge and jury are, my parents Elder and Deaconess Jeramiah and Justine Smith, of the Shine Sanctified Holiness Church. They are one of the founding families of the church and highly respected within their spiritual circle. You could imagine what they felt when I had to tell them that their precious baby girl was pregnant. The immediate shame began. I was an outcast so that's what I was made to feel like. My parents and the old saints had me holding my head down each time I came home to visit from school. It made me feel down, until I had one sister from the church stand up for me. Sister Darlene Magee, she was a beautiful woman you could tell she had a past. When I came home on break, with a protruding belly she immediately took me under her wings. The bond that we had developed allowed me to be focused on myself, my baby, and my faith in God. It helped me with the congregational shame and disgrace I felt.

My parents still today are holding onto the shame that doesn't exist. I'm happy and enjoy the gift that I've been given from God.

Now Jason and me our lives are on to different paths. When Jason graduated, he went home to start to begin his career. So, we Co-Parent and it's working out well.

Chapter 1
Jessica

"Hello, this is Jessica with Johnson Stern Marketing how may I help you?" I was not feeling well today as I answered the direct line to my desk. For the last few months my body has been doing some changes and it's not been for the better.

"Hi, Jessica my name is Matthew Jennings with Showcase Entertainment. This call is to confirm our appointment tonight at the Limelight on 5th."

"Yes Mr. Jennings, we are still on for the meeting at 7:30pm tonight. I will see you there. Thank you for calling to confirm."

I had totally forgotten about the meeting tonight, what am I going to do with Jayce. Let me call my mother quick to see if she can babysit for me. Quick note don't set appointments without confirming a sitter first.

"Hi, mom are you and dad busy tonight? I have a meeting and it's going to run overpass time to pick up Jayce from daycare?"

"Jess, you know I will get my grandbaby. How late are you going to be out; you know he can stay the night."

Yes, that's what I wanted to hear so I can go home and relax after the meeting. I told my mom yes and we said goodnight until tomorrow. I rushed out of the office so I could get freshened up for the meeting with Mr. Jennings. This was an account for his company to advertise throughout the city. The business relationship will be awesome for the firm. I may just get my name recognized in the industry for landing a six-digit client.

Once I got home, I showered and slipped on my go to black dress, some black and gold stilettos with a teal blazer. My accessions were on point. I figured since we were heading to check out the new lounge I could dress and enjoy a dance or two. After I finished getting dressed and headed to the car, I sent over a text for Mr. Jennings of what I was wearing so he wouldn't think I wasn't coming.

"Hello, are you Jessica?"

"Well, who's asking.?" I looked at him and laughed inside. I had already checked his profile out on LinkedIn business site.

I looked up at this 6'2 handsome, peanut butter complexion masculine man, Damn Mr. Jennings, He is sho nuff fine and I know that's not good grammar, but this man is fine.

"If you happen to see Jessica Smith, can you let her know that her client will be sitting at the table over near the wall."

"Well since you put it like that Sir. Hello, I'm Jessica. Nice to meet you."

He shook my hand and asked me to accompany him to the table he had reserved for us. I was a nervous wreck; this was so not my normal. Most clients are older in their mid-60's, this was a first for me. I will be ordering a drink immediately after the pleasantries are done.

We discussed how we can be of service for his business and what he wanted to do in the next six months all the way up to the next 5 years. I can tell he has done his homework on the city and our firm.

I explained what we do at Johnson and Stern, I covered from our history up to the future of Johnson Stern and Smith. You know a girl had to throw a plug in for my potential goals in my career.

Finally, it was over the pleasantries, we settled on another meeting in a week to recap and possibly sign some papers to do business.

Our waitress came over to top off our glasses and take the check. I reached for the check, but Matthew had already taken it. We both said good night. I went deep into the restroom and then went to the bar. I was going to go in hard for at least one drink since I had to drive home.

"What can I get you tonight?" The bartender was handsome; he resembled the guy from Stella who got her groove back.

"Yes, can I get a double shot of Grand Marnier with a slice on the side."

"Bartender, you can place her on my tab."

I heard my tab coming from behind me. When I turned around it was Matthew, was he staying also. He must be checking out the atmosphere while he is making his decision. We sat and drank three more drinks; I was tipsier than I thought once I stopped. I almost stumbled.

When we got outside Matthew offered to give me a ride to my place and leave my car there since I was drinking. I advised him we both needed to catch an Uber because I wasn't riding with him. He smiled at me with those big sexy eyes, no Jessica I have a driver. When the nice black mini limo came around, I hoped to give him my address.

That ride seemed like it was forever, or our conversation was that deep. Once we got to my townhome, I thanked Matthew, and we said good night.

Chapter 2

Jason

I know that this guy didn't just stand up to request a new lawyer, I was working for the cartel and not him. My face fell all the way to the floor. I looked at him as he had lost his mind. This was my fifth pro bono case for the county. You must complete 1500 hours of community service to get a discount on your license. This case was my last one and I would have completed 2100 hours of community service more than enough to get the discount fee.

I asked the judge if I could approach the bench. He granted. The district attorney and I for the case approached the bench. This was a first offense case for jaywalking. I asked the judge if we can have the case dismissed to let this gentleman go. Once the judge looked over at my client, he saw that he was not a threat to anyone and was just possibly in the wrong place at the wrong time when he got the ticket.

All rises said the judge. He dismissed the case and excused everyone. I was so happy and relieved at the same time. You would have thought I was the one who was on trial as I made my way to the court clerk to sign off on my paperwork for the board to get the discount fee.

"Mr. St. John, can you come over and speak with me for a minute. "

"Yes, give me a second to gather my things." I wonder what Washington wants. He was my colleague. We graduated the same time he went to Georgia Tech, and I went to Morehouse. He was from old money, and I was from just getting money.

I caught up to him. He asked if I would be interested in having lunch and discuss a possible career move. You know a brother jumps right on the lunch.

We went over to this Italian spot a few blocks from the courthouse. It was good to have time to eat, relax and catch up and possibly have a chance to make some good money. I have a son who I must prepare for his future, he may one day be recognized as coming from some money.

I'm Jason St. John, from the bayou down south Louisiana. If you noticed my name my roots are Haitian. My great grandfather is from France who came over to Haiti and married a Cuban woman. I'm bi-lingual speaking French, Spanish Creole, and English. My parents and siblings are all fluent in those languages. I was born here in the USA; I didn't learn English until I started school.

I graduated in the top fifty of my class from Morehouse with a degree in Political Science. The time in school was so rewarding, my senior year I managed to fall in love with the most beautiful girl I've ever seen. That relationship was good for me, while at Morehouse. Jessica, she helped me see so much and from a different set of eyes. She had a calming and relaxing personality with a slight wild side. We dated for almost 3 years, which from that time we had s son Jayce Smith-St John. I wanted a Jr, but Jessica refused since she wasn't my wife. She told me that it wouldn't be far to my begotten son. I respected her spiritual choses since I wasn't familiar nor was I trying to get caught up in a spiritual conversation with her. Our relationship ended when Jayce turned 1 year old. I moved back to Florida, and she stayed to complete school. We now co-parent.

"St. John, how has life been treating you." Washington asked. That snapped me back to current.

"It's going well trying to maintain a successful career and get this paper. You know I have a little one I'm working to provide for."

We sat and had lunch catching up. Washington began to open with a proposal of our own practice and how we can make good money with the clients that his father would pass over to him. He said we would be totally successful without any problems. I was floored and then the big question came. I had to ask to be assured I would be around; I sure didn't want to be involved with anything that would get me hurt or harmed in any way. After finally getting the entire truth, it turns out that Washington's family were the attorneys for the mob. Exactly I know you're probably thinking the same as I was. Yes, the mafia, the cartel was who they represented for most of their legal affairs. It would be Washington-St. John Law Firm. The job paid out six figures, starting out with a two hundred-thousand-dollar sign on bonus. The only catch was that I would have to move from Florida to Chicago within the next 30 days. We sat a few minutes longer, shook hands and walked out of the restaurant with smiles of accomplishment on our faces.

I was sitting in my tiny home office leaning back on how I managed to get this far into the events that have transpired in my life this quick. Closing loose ends was my goal. I made a quick checklist to get the ball rolling to relocate. I was thinking of possibly asking Jessica for more time with Jayce since I was going to be more stable financially. He would be able to come and stay the summer or even extended weekends. The key was to convince her to allow him to come to

Chicago, it would be even better if she would come also. I still loved her; it just wasn't our time.

"Hi Jessica, this is Jason when you receive this message. If it's not too late can you give me a call please." I called her so we could discuss my opportunity. Her not answering was not like her. I glanced at the clock and noticed possibly she was putting down Jayce for bed.

I checked around, had a lite snack and drink, and turned in for the evening.

Chapter 3
Shine Sanctified Holiness Church

It's Sunday morning worship time. I rushed in so everyone could see I was on time, since my parents had Jayce. Coming here has been a bittersweet time for me. My heart races every time I come, it's sad but since I had to come in front of these precious perfect saints that do no wrong, I get anxious.

THE CHURCH TRIED TO SHAME ME

Past 3 years Ago

Good Morning Church, before we continue into our services the Smith family would like to stand and give a statement. I was a rising Senior in college and didn't know that this was going down in this manner. My father took the microphone from Elder Gentry and spoke. First, I want to thank God for allowing us to serve you here at Shine Sanctified, where my wife and I are on the board of directors for the church. We are not pleased to make this kind of announcement, but God told us it would be in our best interest to make it publicly known. It appears that sin has come into our home and taken advantage of our daughter Jessica. I was floored, everybody was looking around and all eyes were planted on me. This time I was around 6 six months pregnant, thank goodness I wasn't showing too much. My mother was crying those crocodile tears. She was so dramatic. At that time my father called me up front and made me repent for my sins. I remember it like it was just yesterday. I went up front and stated these exact words.

"Good Morning Church, for those of you who don't know me I'm Jessica Smith, the first daughter of Elder and Deaconess Smith. I've been going here all my life and would consider those of you who are here my church family. As my father has stated, I have sinned and have fallen short on one of the many sins that are listed in the bible and in other minds. If you know God and have an Agape relationship with him 'DON'T COME FOR ME'. I would like for all of you to pray for my parents who have raised and taught me the bible plus morals, respect, and most of all to study or myself. So, since God is the head of my life and the only person I must answer to. I ask that you pray for my parents, my siblings, me, and my unborn child.

I walked to my seat, got my stuff, and went home.

****

I remember that day like yesterday as it is clear in my head. The thought of my parents treating me like some addict. My name is Jessica, and I am a sinner is what it felt like I had said. I was hot with my parents, for making me get up in front of everyone like they were there in the bed with me and Jason.

Now that I was sitting down, I saw Ms. Magee and I moved up to her where I was safe.

The choir was up singing an ole song "look where you brought me from."

Look where he brought me from
Look where he brought me form
Brought me out of darkness
to the marvelous light
Look where he brought me from

That was my song. I loved the way Sis Corrine made it sound like she was singing just for me.

You better sing one of the congregation's members yelled. I was really feeling in a great space this morning. After a few more verses and some praise breaks the preacher got up to preach.

Good morning Saints can we turn to the scripture text today. Turn your bibles to 2 Corinthians 8:10. The sermon covered him speaking on how not to be ashamed of what God has done and doing in your life. He was straight on my lane and all up in my life. This sermon gave me the sense of being in control again and walking with God and not on what others are saying or have to say about me.

Once the preacher finished and my father got up to offer prayer, while the choir was saying.

Here they go again with these songs this morning. My brother was sitting at the keyboards and broke out with Paul Morton's "whatever you're doing in this season".

Lord whatever you're doing in this season
Please don't do it without me
Don't do it without me
(repeat a couple of times)
Lord if you're healing
Healing in the season
Please don't do it without me. Don't do it without me.
Forgiveness in this season > > > > > >

That did it, I was up front before I knew it asking for prayers. I noticed my sister and brother were already standing beside me. My brother was singing this song for me. I had confided in him on several occasions my pain of being accepted with the lives of my parents and not being the outcast. While Sis. Darlene made her way up front and held me like I was her daughter. I loved this lady; she was truly a spiritual mother to me.

Once the song finished my father came up and prayed over the congregation and then he added a few extra words of forgiveness to me without announcing it to everyone. I knew he was speaking to me and asking for my forgiveness. He ended his prayer with Thanks to God and to the pastor for giving us the sermon on not being ashamed and to trust God.

Everyone rushed to their cars after service, but we hung around some since everyone wanted to come and greet me with open arms and hugs. I felt like I had won the lottery, but it's a feeling of God's warmth that I was feeling. I'm so glad my parents had taught me how to love without limits or judgement. Too funny they didn't practice what they preached.

"Hey mommy, I saw you up front crying." My handsome baby was checking on his momma.

"Come over to momma Jayce, I'm alright baby. Did you have fun with Grandma and Grandpa?" He stayed over the entire weekend with them upon my mother's request.

You see I had limited the time with them since I wasn't welcomed over as much since I got pregnant with Jayce. Ms. Darlene opened her home for me and Jayce until I found an apartment for us. Yes, you heard it, the Spiritual Saints my parents wouldn't let me come home with a baby. I wasn't allowed to bring him into their home without a husband.

Jason gave me child support for Jayce, and I saved all my student aid checks until I found a place that Ms. Darlene would agree for us to be safe in.

"Hi MiMi baby, Ms. Darlene said to Jayce. "he pulled my hand and asked if he could go over to MiMi and hug her tight. Yes, go ahead but don't run or jump up on her.

Once everyone showed me love, my mother came over and hugged me. She whispered in my car how sorry she was and asked me to forgive her. I whispered back to Momma I already did 3years ago. We hugged tighter and I kissed her, told her I love her.

"Momma, Momma! Can we go to MiMi house for dinner today?" That little fellow who knew of mine loved his MiMi mac and cheese.

"Jayce, we are going to eat at home. Is that alright with you since you're the man of the house."

"Momma, you don't have mac and cheese or homemade cornbread like MiMi."

Everybody looked at me and Darlene and burst out laughing. I wasn't laughing because he was correct, I didn't have it and didn't know how to make it either. You see I didn't know a lot of cooking since we ate out most of my childhood.

"Jayce, MiMi got your Sunday box in the car baby." I gave her the side eye.

We said our goodbyes, and everyone departed the church parking lot.

Chapter 3

Jessica

Mondays are always not my friend; it seems like it's always going slow. This Monday wasn't any different. Jayce was still asleep; something must not be right. He is usually up or at least his TV is blasting out cartoons. I walked in his room; this little boy was still in a deep sleep. I reached for him, and he was soaking wet from his head to his little feet. This can't be happening to us.

Jayce baby woke up, I called out to him. He moved slightly. My baby little head was burning up. I reached for his thermometer while calling the doctor's office at the same time. My baby had a fever of almost 105.; I almost passed out from fear. I pulled him out of the bed thank goodness I had already gotten dressed.

We arrived at the doctor's office in 0.5 seconds, they were expecting us.

Hi, Ms. St. John, how are you, bring Jayce back, we are waiting on him. Once they checked his vitals my baby had gone in and out. I heard sirens; they were very faint. I turned around to see that it was the ambulance in the building. Dr. Keziah came over and said to Ms. St. John we are going to have to transport Jayce over to the hospital. It sounds like he has a severe respiratory virus or infection. His fever has me worried so we need to admit him, you can ride over with him please to keep him calm.

I was a nervous wreck. I called my parents, Ms. Darlene, Jason, and my job. Finally, after three hours which it only took Ms. Darlene 2 minutes to arrive at the hospital, Lord knows I think she is an angel, and she will be on the scene within seconds of everything. When I had Jayce, she almost beat me and Jason to the hospital.

I was called back to be with Jayce, my little man was hooked up to all kinds of machines. I immediately prayed over my baby.

Dear Father, it's me Jessica please take care of my baby. You're a healer and comforter, allow him not to suffer or be in any pain. We are ready to receive this lesson, an adventure that you are bestowing upon us. Father, you're the original doctor. Lend the doctors and the staff here in this hospital to be knowledgeable in taking care of my baby. I pray for him and myself to be strong. In your son Jesus name, I pray. AMEN.

That moment his machines started to beep beeping and making loud noises. It was getting louder and louder. It continued and I was asked to step out of the room. I walked out crying, Lord please send your angels to surround and protect my baby.

When I got back into the waiting room. I was crying hysterically, Ms. Darlene, and my mother ran to me at the same time. My father said give her some room, you too are going to make her sick, going to have both my babies in the room together.

I went out to the hall from the waiting room and ran into Matthew. I was surprised to see him there looking at me with those big eyes. I smiled a brief second; it gave me a sense of relief.

"Hi Jessica, what are you doing here?" he asked me.

"Hi Matthew, my son is here in the children's ER. I came out here to get some air."

"Do you need anything? My brother is a Pediatrician doing his residency here. We just had lunch. I wonder if it was your son that they just paged on about?

"Oh really, yes my son machines just went crazy so it's possible."

He followed me to the waiting area since I couldn't shake him. When I got back to the waiting area my mother and Ms. Darlene was both gone. I knew either they were in the chapel or had to get some air. Seated were my father, my siblings and Jason had arrived.

"Hi Jessica, how are you holding up? I arrived a few minutes ago. The doctors are still with him and not allowing anyone to go back yet."

"Yes, I was back when the equipment went off and they kicked me out.' Tears fell down my face.

"I'm here now, we will be able to go back soon." Jason was giving Matthew the side eye.

"Thanks Jason, I know we will be able to go back there. This is Matthew Jennings, my colleague, his brother is the pediatrician on duty." I could see Jason looking crazy.

Late into the night I had dozed off laying on Jason's shoulder. When the doctor came in to talk with us. He explained that Jayce has a severe upper respiratory infection with possible meningitis. According to documents a child at the learning center had the virus and it must have been passed on to several of the children at the center. We will be keeping him until we can get his fever under control. We will allow his parents to see him tonight since he is heavily sedated.

Once he is clear to a normal fever, we will allow other visitors at the parents' consent.

They allowed me and Jason to go back to see him.

We went back to see him, and he was sleeping still hooked up to the machines.

I broke down and cried while Jason was trying to hold me. We both leaned down on the bed and cried. We started to pray for our baby.

My baby started to move; he opened his eyes briefly. His little voice said momma I'm okay don't cry. My baby fell back off to sleep. We sat there for a few more minutes.

I went back out to the waiting room and gave everyone some brief information and advised them to go home since Jayce would be alright. We hugged everyone good night.

"Jessica, do you need a ride to your car? "Jason asked.

"Oh, no I didn't drive. I rode in the ambulance with Jayce. My car is still at the doctor's office."

"Jason, if you don't mind can you give me a ride home. I can pick my car up tomorrow."

The ride was quick. Before I knew it, we were already at my house. Jason, would you like to come in? If you haven't had a chance to stop at a hotel you are more than welcome to stay here. I can give you some blankets for the sofa or you are welcome to sleep in Jayce's room. He took me up on the offer. We both showered and were sitting in the living room. I offered him a drink and we sat and caught up for a while, before I knew it, we had drunk an entire bottle of Crown Royal Apple. I told Jason I was going to bed, I felt myself stumble in the hall. Jason ran and caught me. He had to help me to the bedroom, I fell on the bed real hard, I pulled Jason down towards my face and started kissing him. We both became locked in a tongue fight with our mouths. It had been almost a year since I had been with or allowed a man to touch me. I wanted to have him next to me. We continued to kiss. He had his hands rubbing all over my thighs while we were kissing. I felt my body shaking on the inside from his touch. He had his fingers inside my vagina oh my goodness I was soaking wet. I laid back and whispered to Jason, I want you, inside of me". He kissed me and slid up over top of me putting his fingers inside me to make sure I was wet. I felt the tip of his hard erection. I jumped and moaned; he asked me should he stop. I pulled him down into me. No Jason don't stop. We went at it for twenty-five more minutes and we both climaxed together, I fell off to sleep in his arms.

Chapter 4

Jason

Thanks, Washington. I appreciate you considering me as a partner. It's going to be a great opportunity for me. I'm excited to take on this adventure in my career.

We spent the time making calls and setting up appointments the week prior to moving into our new office. The grand opening would be next week, and we are going to take walk-in clients.

Moving up here to Chicago will be a new beginning for me. The weather up here I hope it's gentle to me.

I came into town and found a nice lakefront condo flat. I spent about 300K on the purchase, furniture for my new place.

I rolled over the sky was clear white and the lake was white. The room was freezing, I didn't want to go to the bathroom. I hopped out the bed and turned the setting for the floor warmer to come on for 20 mins. My eyes had to be playing tricks on me. I knew it wasn't snowing in early spring.

"Hi Jason, can you come now Jayce is at the hospital he was running a high fever." Before Jessica could hang up good. I was on my way to the airport to charter a private jet to go to my baby boy. Well, he is almost 4 years old not a baby, but he is my baby.

I told Jessica I would be there. During the plane ride I was tearing up. I hadn't seen Jayce in about 6 months with my new job trying to get settled.

It surprised me to hear from Jessica since I had called her over a month ago and she hadn't returned my call. She had reverted to just simple text messages as I was just a baby daddy. I still loved her and hope that she will soon marry me once I'm able to provide for her and Jayce. Taking this job to Chicago was the best move that can lead me on the way for success.

I arrived at the hospital to find Jessica not in the waiting room and no one knew where she was since the doctors told her to leave the room while they tended to Jayce.

Here she is in the arms of another man. I could feel my blood boiling who this guy Jessica is with. Is she dating, she can't have this man around our son? My mind was in a total I'm jealous mood.

She introduced him as a work colleague. I was relieved.

The doctor came and we were able to go back and see our son. It was a relief to know that Jayce would be alright, and it was now awaiting process. We would have to let them do their job for the night.

My mind went to relax and relax. Jessica prayed over our son, and he woke up enough to tell her that he was okay. We stayed long enough for him to drift back off to sleep.

I was glad Jessica offered her place since I hadn't secured a hotel yet. We hadn't spoken on a staying over the night occasion, so I didn't want to impose on him.

We showered and relaxed. I had almost forgotten how smooth and calming her voice was when she spoke. This may be the time to tell her that I want my family back. She offered me a drink and we talked most of the night until we had nothing left to drink. Jessica was tipsy and so cute the first day I met her. Those big eyes and that warm smile. We said good night so we could sleep before getting up to head back to the hospital.

Before I could get it out that Jessica you're falling, I was already catching her in the hallway. Yes, held on like it was the end of the world. She kissed me before I knew it, we were entwined as one making love like we hadn't ever been apart. I moved and she kept up with every move I made. Her plea of having me inside her I was glad to give her what she wanted and needed as well as myself.

We had twenty-five minutes of serious love making. I grabbed onto her, and we both fell asleep.

Chapter 5

Jessica

OMG, I tried to roll over but couldn't. My body felt like I had been beaten. Why can't I move, am I dreaming? I moved again and noticed I was being held in some strong masculine arms.

I pulled the arms from around me and made my way to the restroom. What did I do last night, my memory serves me that Jayce was resting in the hospital? I invited Jason over to stay for the night since he arrived and came straight to the hospital. I know we had a drink and now I'm waking up with a terrible headache, my body ache and I'm half naked. I immediately prayed.

"Good Morning, Beautiful how did you sleep?" Jason was sitting on the edge of the bed when I came out of the restroom. He is to dang sexy, I sure missed him. The memories of us being together during school. We would have so much fun, laughing and talking. Now we are just co-parenting Jayce in our own separate lives. Last night was a blur to me. I hope he tells me without me having to ask.

"Good Morning, Handsome. Yes, I slept well, just not sure how you got in my room and not in Jayce or on the sofa? "I gave him a serious not serious look, hoping that he would tell me. Sitting here looking at Jason I see so much of our son. He holds his head the same way when he is thinking. He has that same sneaking smile when he is beginning to tell a lengthy response or lie.

WOW I didn't realize how many similarly he has like his father.

"Jessica, are you telling me you don't remember getting me drunk and taking advantage of me last night? "

"I'm serious, Jason I feel like crap, I'm not wearing any panties and I think I see a few passion marks on my chest and around your neck. So, Mr. St. John, what is your defense."

We both laughed, I was trying to sound like an attorney. While Jason began to tell me how innocent our sexual episode happened last night, I made us a small breakfast.

Having a few more laughs we both got up and showered. Jason dropped me off to pick up my car and we headed over to the hospital to see our baby.

When we arrived at the hospital, my parents, Ms. Darlene was waiting in. Oh, we thought you had forgotten to call us, they all said in unison. I continued to walk like I didn't hear them. My mother of course kept on talking. Jessica, what took you so long to get here. Jessica why didn't you call us and tell us where on the way. Finally, my father said. Justine close your mouth sometimes; this isn't your business. You should try staying in your place. You see that our baby is trying to hold onto her sanity while her child is in here hooked up to those machines. Justine shut up and prayed for our daughter and grandson.

I was floored that daddy finally stood up to momma. He grabbed me and hugged me. Daddy loves you baby, I'm sorry. We all walked in silence until we got inside the hospital.

I was shocked to see Matthew standing there. Why is he here again today, does his brother really work for her or is he stalking?

"Hi Jessica and Jason, how are you both doing this morning?

"Hi Matthew." Jason answered for us.

I'm still confused why Matthew is here again today.

"Bruh, what up you ready? I heard a similar voice. turning around I felt like I was looking at a darker version of Matthew. That must be his brother he was speaking about last night.

"Hi, Mark. I thought I was going to eat alone today. Oh, this is Jason and Jessica, I was telling you about their son from yesterday."

"Hi Mrs. and Mrs. St. John, how are you both doing today? Go ahead to see Jayce, I'm on my way to have lunch we can talk once I get back.

"Thank you."

Me and Jason went in to see Jayce. My heart was beating so fast with anticipation.

"Mommy Mommy, I heard my baby saying. He was off the machines sitting up watching TV when we walked into the room. I broke down crying tears of joy.

"Mommy way are you crying, I told you I was going to be alright."

"Oh, Jayce momma is crying because I'm so happy."

"Hey there son."

"Hi Daddy"

The three of us sat on the bed hugging each other. I stayed with Jayce while Jason went back out to give my parents a full report. That gave me a chance to talk with Jayce, catching up on his memory of events.

Jayce gave me a play by play of what happened to him from Wednesday until today. This young man has a memory of an elephant as the old folks would say. He informed me that his friend Marcia had a cough and her mother picked her up early. The ride him and his grandma made to Sonic to get a smoothie that he loved so much. Note to self to take to momma about all those sugary treats. He said he felt bad after church when we were eating, but he wanted to play and didn't tell me he was sick. Finally, he told me that he felt me talking to him in the ambulance and my prayers he heard them. I told him momma loved him. He said one more thing mommy, I saw three angels, they told me I was doing a great job as the man of the house. He continued to tell me how he was going to be the man of the house until his sister that he picked out would be ready to come from heaven.

Jayce alright that's enough, once I said that the nurse was coming in to give him his medicine. This little boy has a memory and an imagination. I just sat with him until he drifted off to sleep in my arms.

Back in the waiting room when I got out everyone was sitting watching TV. I brought them up to date on the events of what happened and that they can go see him for only 15 minutes. Since he was asleep that was good, he wouldn't become exhausted, and they can go home and rest.

Jason came over to inform me that he would be checking into a hotel, to be safe from me. We laughed but knew that would be best since the focus was on Jayce not us.

Everyone had left and I was sitting in the lounge chair in Jayce's room. I had all my calls forwarded to the answering service; my assistant rescheduled all my appointments a week out.

Dr. Mark Jennings came to update me on Jayce. It will be another two days then possibly my baby can come home. He has fought the infection off, now its observation to assure no hidden complications.

Chapter 6

Deaconess Justine Smith

I had to hurry; I'm running behind as usual. Every second Thursday night we have our deaconess and lady's ministry meeting. With the events that's happened this week, I really need to see my sisters for prayer.

Walking across the parking lot, I could feel the eyes on me. Since we started this work our lives have been on a fast pace. I had my doubts, but we have been at this for almost thirty years.

I've had to be a standing example for the women in this congregation for years. Our lives must be perfect. In my earlier days before I met Jeremiah, I had a terrible past. When he met me, I was on my second failed relationship and fourth pregnancy scare. He saved my life. My parents didn't care about what I did or who I did it with. One of my friends from chorus asked me to go to her youth group seminar for the weekend. I agreed just to get out of the house for a weekend, I met Jemimah, he was the popular guy that every girl wanted to be his girl, he was a church celebrity. During this trip I told Melissa my friend that I wanted to just have fun. Little did I know that I had a chance to find out who Jesus was, how much he loved me and meet plenty of young adults who loved themselves like Jesus loved them.

One night I slipped off to get high. I had stolen some wine from my parent's wine cellar, a few joints that my brother had in his stash. My goal was to get high before we had to head back home. Guess who also out roaming Jeremiah Smith was, like he was on a mission for God to seek out all sinners.

"Announce yourself or get your head blown off." I said with a bold stern voice.

"How did you get a weapon past, Elder Jones."

"Announce yourself, I started and made a click noise with my mace case."

"Alright, don't shoot. I'm Jeramiah Smith from the Temple of God church. Please don't' shoot me God has work for me to do."

I told him he could take down his hands and walk over to me slowly. When he got over to me, he grabbed me and started kissing me. I pushed him back off me.

"Mr. Smith, do you walk around in the woods at night kissing people? Is this a habit you have:" If you do then we might need for Elder Jones to pray for you?"

He laughed at me, which made me laugh. I told him that he was interrupting my going home ritual that I had just thought of before we left. He asked if he could join me to listen, since he didn't drink or smoke. I allowed him to watch as I became an intoxicated horny woman. Here I was in the woods with a handsome young man, and he isn't trying to feel me up or get into my panties. That night for the first time in my young adult life I felt in control, respected, and loved.

We talked and laughed all night. I'm not sure how long or what happened after the last memory was Elder Jones and Sister Jones waking us up. I was ashamed, embarrassed that we were caught. Jeremiah took the blame for the weed and alcohol. He later told me that he didn't want to bring any problems or for anyone to find out. His explanation was he had to protect his future wife from any disgrace and shame.

Snapping back to current date>>>> I am going to have to make this right. How could I have gone along with the other members in making my own child feel ashamed for deciding that she shouldn't have been ashamed of.

———————————————————————————————————————

Let's get the meeting started Sister Mills, made the announcement. We have an upcoming Ladies event and need to get it rolling quick. If papers that the pastor is wanting us to go in direction to sustain the younger generation. In his words we need to be reverent to what is happening in the world today.

Now stop all that whispering, give some ideas please instead of some unwanted critics. If we lose the young adults the church will die. Sis Darlene stood up, with a suggestion of Walking in Authority or I am Not My Sin. We had a few more suggestions that can be great eye catchers for the Ladies Day Event.

Sis Mills asked that we use our own congregation members to be speakers to save money, as well as keep the young adults involved. Once we discussed more details and who we could consider asking to speak.

"Sis Smith, do you think that Jessica can speak to our college bound ladies?"

I quickly jolted a look at Sis Darlene; she has always been in my face about how I worshipped Jessica instead of loving her. How dare she ask that in front of everyone. I rolled my eyes at her when no one was looking.

"Yes, Sis Smith that will be a great idea. She would be a blessing to some of the youth that may consider college but had a minor setback.' Sis Mills stated.

From that point I began to boil. Then up Sister Winston. She spoke softly and we had to ask her to speak up a little. Well sisters I'm asking for your prayers while my household is experiencing some disappointment in Rachel. She had been running away for the last three months. Come to find out she was over her boyfriends' home, his parents thought we had put her out because she is six months pregnant. Before I knew it, I was holding her hand while she sobbed.

I stood up and said let's keep the Winston's in prayer for the right way to handle this as God would see fit. Let's be a help to her and Rachel during this time. We all know that I was in a similar situation with Jessica that has bruised our relationship. So, let's pray for the Winston's to be restored to help Rachel because she needs her family and church at this time.

I agreed to asking Jessica to speak; we all agreed on the items discussed, prayed, and went home.

When I sat in the car, I prayed that God lead me, guide me, to help me heal from this mess I've created between me and Jessica.

Three Months Later:.......

The events that transpired over the last three months have begun healing for everyone. I brought Jayce home; we jumped back into our routine life. Jason and I have decided to continue our co-parenting. Then for our relationship we decided to try this long distance to see how it would work and if we should decide on who would relocate. From the couple of nights, we made love and spent time as a family. He professed his love for me and asked if I could give him a second chance.

On my return-to-work Mr. Jennings signed a 2-year contract. He also suggested I try to venture out on my own soon. That was great. I had already considered doing just that. Everyone should have their own business.

My mother had come to me regarding our relationship. She wanted to know if I would speak to young adults at a program for the ladies' group. I was shocked and confused. Before I took the challenge, I asked my mother why. Once she mentioned Ms. Darlene, I blocked her out, and said yes to the opportunity.

This was my chance to use my speaking skills and perhaps be a blessing to someone like me 4 years ago. The event was a success and I signed up for many more that would be like some help to young girls and women in conflict of being accepted through their personal sins.

Chapter 7
Jason

Thanks for meeting me today, Mr. Calhoun, we can discuss your case before the court date. It appears that you are on video with your face looking directly into the camera. This is your first offense; I've gone to the DA and asked to have the charges dismissed. To no avail they declined, stating they have ties to Juan Gomez family. So, Mr. Calhoun, what is your take on this matter?

He replied straight up that he was at the wrong place at the wrong time. That he is willing to take a plea to get it behind him since he is dating Mr. Gomez's niece. I advised him to come back into the office around 4 o'clock pm.

We talked briefly, and I excused him to make a call to the DA to work out a decent deal.

I made a few more calls and left a message for Rebecca Jenson, the criminal Defense Attorney for the superior court. She was a beautiful Canadian, French African American woman, tall, nice complexion, and a body like Iman the model. She was fine, our run-ins were so intense, but we had a great working relationship. Rebecca was fine and I wanted to embrace her but that was so unprofessional. Let me get back to matters at hand.

"Hello, Rebecca, how are you doing today? This is St. John. I wanted to chat about the Calhoun case." I'm hoping she remembers the name without having to place me on a long hold.

"Well St. John, how are you doing? Haven't heard from you in a while. We must get lunch real soon."

"Yes, that would be great real soon."

"I have considered the case against Mr. Calhoun, since you put it that it's his first offense and according to the way he was looking at the camera as if he was just a regular customer and not involved with the crime that was taking place on the other side of the store. We can dismiss the case. By the way St. John, you owe me. I'll be waiting for that lunch sooner than later."

"Sure Jensen, I'll call you."

WE both shared a laugh, us using last names was a game we played while serving on a volunteer team with the local College coaching the paralegal students. That was great she dropped those charges this will be great news to the Gomez family and for Calvin Calhoun

I had a few minutes to waste so I called Jessica since my mind was playing tricks on me. My manhood had been jumping around in my pants during the entire conversation with Rebecca.

While dialing Jessica's number I was getting a text from Washington reminding me of our upcoming trip to Columbia in a few weeks. I clicked read so he would know I didn't ignore the message but read it.

Jessica's voicemail came on, so I left her a message to call me when she was free; and I gave my love to her and Jayce.

Thanks for coming back to Mr. Calhoun, hello Maria it's good to see you. I wanted to inform you that all charges are dropped, and you are free to go. I have a few documents drawn up for you to sign just see my secretary when you leave. Maria was crying, after hearing that her fiancé was free of all charges to go. He reached out his hand to shake and Maria hugged me with a large hug. Calvin walked towards the door and reached inside his pocket and gave me an envelope. Maria says thank you, she said they would name their first male child after me which was due in 4 months. I again said thank you and they left.

Today was a long day. I couldn't wait to get home shower and relax. Being your own boss was great but exhausting. What is it they say hard work does pay off?

While I was walking out of the office the phone rang, not now. I just allowed the answering service to pick it up and left.

I summoned the car to dial Jessica again, I knew she would be home at this hour. It rang for a while then finally I heard my young man say Hi, Daddy. When are you coming to see me, I miss you and I know mommy does too? That was the sweetest thing ever. We talked a while then I asked him to put his mom on the line.

"Hey Jess, I love you and miss you so much. Would you marry me? It was a silence in the air after I said that. "Jess, Jess are you there." Did this woman hang up on me, was my thoughts?

I waited for a while and the phone went dead.

I tried to call right back but it went straight to voicemail. I was leaving a voice message and my phone rang.

"Jason, I apologize I dropped the phone. Did you say what I think you said?"

"Yes Jess, and I meant it. Would you be honored to be my wife? I knew that it's not the traditional way but when I see you, I'll put this ring on your finger. It's in your text messages. So, what's your answer?"

"Jason yes I would love to be your wife." I love you.

We chatted for a few more minutes and ended the call with a good night.

These last few weeks had been long. The reward of being an entrepreneur was great. Living here in Chicago hasn't been at all bad to me. I'm sure Jessica and Jayce will love it here. It would be best for me to convince her to relocate since I'm already established, and she can open her own Global Marketing Firm. I will be sure to mention it when I fly down to see them this weekend.

"Good Morning Mr. St. John, your first appointment is already in your office waiting. They insisted on waiting in your office."

"Thank you." I didn't have a client who could be here to see me and insisting on being in my office.

I walked in from the side door, with my briefcase in tow. My eyes were locked on two large men in nice Italian suits standing at the door. In the chair facing my desk were two beautiful women, I'm not sure if they were Brazilian or Columbian. I had to do a double take; they were twins.

"Good morning, I'm Jason, how may I help you?"

"Hi, Jason, we are the Cruz Twins, I'm Carmen and this is Camilla. We need your legal services for an Emancipation from our parents."

These two young ladies were under the age of 18 years of age, trying to separate themselves from their parents.

"Well young ladies I want to say, I'm honored that you would consider me as your attorney. Can you tell me how you heard about me?

The girls went on to tell me how they heard of me, why they chose me, and the biggest shocker was who their parents were. Hearing their stories and reasons. I explained to them that I would accept their case only if we would have mediation first. They were pleased with the mediation, but it must happen. They left me an envelope on the table, gave me a handshake and left out.

I had to pour myself a strong stiff drink. They're in my office at the competition, children wanting to divorce their parents. Omg I am going to need to consult with Washington on this one how could I've been put in this kind of mess. I wonder if the Gomez boys at the Cruz attorney are asking the same thing. This is going to be something I can't wait to see.

I managed to survive the week. First thing when I pulled up to my condo, I got showered and went straight to bed. My flight would be leaving at 5am head out Georgia.

Chapter 8
Jessica

Come on Jayce we must hurry so we won't be late. Your daddy is arriving in another hour we must leave. Getting this young man up has been a struggle for me, he's definite his father's son. Jason wouldn't get up when we would fall asleep. I'm so glad that we never got caught; we would have both been banned from the campus. We both ran out the door to leave.

It was hot outside today; this Georgia heat is crazy. When arrived at the gate just in time to see Jason walking out to the walk up. I honked and he got in the car, smelling so good. He gave me a kiss and Jayce high five.

He was looking so fine, in some nice True Religion jeans a custom button-down French cuff shirt with a tweed two-toned blazer. This man had on some alligator boots, in this HOT Georgia weather.

"Jason, I'm feeling the look. Is that how attorneys from the big city dress?"

"Real Funny Jess, this outfit is not over the top is it? I just didn't want to travel in a 3-piece suit."

From the back Jayce says momma daughter looks handsome and those boots I want a pair for me just like daddy.

We rode to the house, laughing, and catching up since the last time we saw each other.

I pulled into my garage; Jayce had fallen asleep in no time. Jason carried him to his room. I went to the restroom to come out to Jason down on one knee with a blue box in his hand. He was looking at me with those handsome eyes.

"Jessica Smith, will you marry me?"

"Yes, Jason Yes." I said with my hand out. He pushed up the ring on my finger. I had to take a second look. It was a 5-carat princess cut diamond with a diamond clustered band.

"Jason, this is beautiful."

I leaned down to kiss him, I felt my entire body shake. My heart was pounding, and I was so excited we were going to be married. Become a family!

From that moment I felt complete. While kissing I felt his hands under my sundress, pulling my panties to the side. He brushed his fingers on my opening, to slide his fingers inside of my wetness. Jason, I love you, I moaned. He kissed me and pulled my panties completely off, while I was unbuttoning his pants. I could see the bulging in his pants, I pulled his pants off to his boxer only. We caressed one another as we slowly became one. Jason had taken off his boxers and my panties. Our rhythm was as one, we loved each other like it was our first time ever. This played on for about another thirty minutes until we fell off to sleep.

Later that night, I made dinner. I prepared some Cuban Red Snapper, Yellow Rice with Peas, Fried Cabbage, and Carrots with Plantains. When we sat down, Jason said something in French Maudite femme tu vas rendre un homme fou, comment tu sais que c'était mon préféré.

Damn fanm nou pwal fè yon moun fou, jan ou konnen sa li te genyen m' ke (Haitian).

I laughed and said Oui je sais, vous rendre fou, Jason votre déjà fou.

I looked at me and said oh, so you remember. I winked at him. We said the blessing and all three of us ate.

Once we finished dinner, Jason Face timed his parents to tell them the news and so they could see Jayce. I didn't speak French so I couldn't communicate with them. I had to have Jason to translate. They gave us their blessings and said they would come to the wedding and how excited they were.

We turned it in early since we had a big day tomorrow. My parents didn't know so we wanted to tell them in person. So, I planned a brunch at the Midnight Diner to tell them our news.

Good Morning beautiful, Jason was staring at me. Baby what is wrong why are you looking at me that way. He told me how much he loved me and his plans to have us come to Chicago to visit for a few days to see how we would like to relocate. It was great to hear him with the plans for his family. We had another love making session and got up to get dressed. While Jason was in the shower, I had gone to check on Jayce. This young man is sound asleep. I'm going to let his father handle this. I placed his clothes out, gave him a kiss, and tiptoed out.

I jumped into the shower while Jason was getting out. Can you go and see if Jayce is up; I don't want him to be rushing.

I finished up, got out of the shower, and was dressed ready to go. I was starving and couldn't wait to get some of those famous Shrimp and Grits. When I walked into the living room, their sitting on the sofa was Jayce and Jason both looking at me like I was taking too long. Something wasn't right. I looked at them and folded my hands.

"Jayce, did you dad have to wake you up.""

"No mommy has a clock that sings to me. It says my name and tells me to wake up. I turned it off and got my shower and put my clothes on like you and daddy taught me."

I was puzzled. I didn't see no clock in his room. Was he just telling me this, I will have to investigate this tonight the two of them are up to something?

When I arrived for brunch, my parents, Ms. Darlene and to my surprise were Jason's parents. He is so sneaky I should have noticed the backdrop on FaceTime last night, but I didn't pay attention to the details. I was happy to see everyone; we sat and ordered our food. Once we were almost finished eating. Jason stood up gathering everyone's attention.

"Family, we are glad that everyone could join us for this brunch this morning. (He had to translate minimally for his parents). He motioned for me and Jayce to stand up with him.

"Mom & Dad, Mr. & Mrs. Smith and Ms. Darlene I would like to have your blessing. I've asked Jayce if it was alright that me and his mother get married."

I showed them my ring after the tears and congratulations were under control. Everyone came over for hugs. We continued to eat while sitting for the wedding.

Tonight, was so beautiful.

Chapter 9
Matthew Jennings

So little brother are you going to tell me about that young lady whose son I was treating at the hospital.

My mind was preoccupied deep in thought when I heard my brother talking but not hearing the words that were coming from his mouth. He shoved me.

"Matt, come on man you know you hear me. Who is the young lady from the hospital? I could tell she has your heart.

"Well, your partially correct Mark, she is a colleague from a marketing firm that I met with about some advertising. I didn't have a chance to get to know her personally until I saw her at the hospital. She is already spoken for. IT's going to be only business now."

"Matt, just be careful little brother I don't want you to be hurt."

I continued to think of Jessica a moment. Why didn't I ask her all those need-to-know questions prior to seeing her at the hospital? Mark was right, my heart was a little bruised.

I took a moment to say a prayer to god for direction, guidance and understanding in this situation.

"Good Morning thank you for calling Showcase Entertainment, this is Matthew how can I help you."

"Well Mr. Jennings, you are pulling double duty today?

Hearing Jessica's voice sent me into a deep daze. I didn't hear anything that she was saying. Why am I having these un pure thoughts of her. Why am I in love with this woman, whom I don't really know? She was still talking when I heard my name........

"Matthew, Matthew can you hear me?

"Oh, I'm sorry Jessica my phone was on mute, I heard you. Yes, I'm prepared to go over the documents at your earliest convenience. I also have a proposal for you for another opportunity."

"Sure Matthew, let's meet this coming week to finalize and discuss the new opportunity."

After ending the call with Jessica, I needed to go cool off. I pulled up to the gym for a few laps in the pool then off to relax at home.

You can Write Personal Notes:

Have you ever been made to feel ashamed for a sin you committed?

Were you able to recover from that guilt?

Do you think Christ allows these Sins to happen to build up your Faith?

Chapter 10
Jason

Daddy, Daddy please don't leave I want you to stay with us. I need you here to help me take care of mommy. It tore me up to see Jayce crying, ever since his health scare this little guy has become such a mature young man. Telling me how much he loves his mother and will be taking care of her. He even mentioned that he picked out a sister to come from heaven to join our family. This made me think of the old saying from the ole country that my grandmother used to say that children can see what we can't.

I reassured him that I would be back soon for him and his mother to come to Chicago after my trip.

"Jason, when are you going on your trip to Columbia? Will you please send me the information of your trip since it's a third world country? We will be in Chicago at your place when you arrive back."

"I love you Jessica you're such a beautiful strong woman. When I return from this trip, I can't wait to make you my wife."

I kissed my family, told them how much I loved them and hurried to catch my plane.

Once I got back in Chicago the weather had done a complete 180. It was colder than when I left, hopefully this weather will change back to a normal temperature or at least in between the north pole and equator soon.

"Good Morning, Washington how was your weekend?"

"Oh, it was great how about you, was your trip good? Did you get turned down gently?"

"No, she said," Yes, you know I am the man." I said with a smile. He knew Jessica is the love of my life, but my goals had to be met before I could ask him to marry me. Unlike him I wasn't financially fit to have a puppy. So, I wanted to secure my career at least that I could afford to provide for her and Jayce.

Washington was already married. He married his high school sweetheart. I always tease him it was an arranged marriage.

"So, Washington have you considered what we should do with the Cruz girls?" This matter would need to be handled before we leave for the trip. I set up a mediator to come in if one is needed.

"St. John, man that was so crazy I had never had or heard of anything like this before. Did you contact their father like I suggested?"

"Yes, Man I sure did. I contacted both sets of parents, to my surprise they both already knew that they girl and boys were trying to bring them together."

Me and Washington agreed to meet with the parents and then bring in the children. Turns out that when I met with them, they were considered to join forces since they offered to separate products. That was a win for all parties involved. Now the Gomez and Cruz families are partners.

During the remainder of the week, I was busy and I was ready to leave for the trip. This is a one-time venture just to show an American face with the building we are securing, for the Gomez and Cruz Cartel. This is going to be a walk in the park easy three-day trip.

We discussed a little more of the arrangements and were ready to leave tomorrow morning.

Hey Washington, one more thing on the trip to tomorrow. I set up a meeting with a new Cartel family. They're in need of Canadian counsel and wanted to secure someone that knows the business. I thought we could use some extra spending money. It would have been selfish of me to not include you since you're starting a new family. That nice suburb home is going to cost you a good ½ or 1 million in Chicago. We will see.

We ended our day. I came in to call my family and then to get prepared for my trip.

"Hey Jessica, I sure miss you already. Is Jayce still up? Yes, I wanted to tell him goodnight before he goes to bed."

"Hi baby, I sure miss you too. Yah he's almost asleep."

Me and Jayce talked for about thirty minutes about when they came to Chicago. I loved his thoughts; how courteous he is.

'Jessica, I mailed you all the details of my trip along with the key to the condo. I love you I'll see you soon."

We talked until we fell asleep on one another. In another week I will be holding both of my babies.

Chapter 11
Jessica

If I must go into one more bridal shop I am going to just fall out. We should have just had a in the middle of the living room wedding, our immediate family there was enough for me. I had enough, this was the last store. Alright everyone this is a wrap; I have made my decision. This has become too much for me. I told my mother, and Ms. Darlene I chose a dress from a small boutique in Conyers, GA. The look on their faces was priceless. I was tickled inside.

Well Ms. Jessica Smith-St John to be, you could have told us that on store number two. I'm starving. Let's get a snack and a drink. I second that Darlene lets go, I need a real strong drink.

Did I just hear these two correctly? They said let's get a snack and a drink. Waking behind them I was laughing.

The remainder of the week was easy. I handled all my appointments, got all contracts signed. My last meeting was with Matthew and it's close to home which was great. Tonight, I allowed Jayce to stay with Ms. Darlene since we would be flying out in a few days. She was on the list for his school so she could take him or call in and keep him home with her.

I freshened up, preparing for my meeting with Matthew. For some reason I've been feeling a warmth come over me when his name is mentioned, or his face comes into my mind. Hopefully our meeting will help ease this feeling or make it clear why I'm getting this feeling. From our last encounter at the hospital, I could see something may have been bothering him after seeing me and Jason together. Trust me I will get to the bottom of it.

I finished getting dressed. I chose to wear something business casual, taking that Chicago approach like Jason wore. I had on some NY&CO boot cut jeans, with a plum and pink French cuff blouse, and my boot style stiletto heels. Sprayed a little of the Kat von D perfume and breezed out the door. I know this deal is a go.

I headed out the door to meet with Matthew. This wasn't going to be an all-night meeting, get in handle things, hear his new proposal and home for a long hot bubble bath. I didn't have to pack. I had all our bags ready.

I walked in the Dessert Bar, my eyes locked on Matthew at the bar.

Hi Mr. Jennings, I spoke to him with his back turned. He turned around, quickly with a handsome smile.

Jessica how are you tonight? You look lovely.

We sat and talked about some of what has been happening business related for an hour. He agreed and signed the contract to work with our firm. There was even a bonus check for me enclosed in the envelope. He paid the ticket, and we began to leave the restaurant.

"Jessica, I wanted to show you the new business opportunity. It's overheard inside the business center."

I followed behind him to see what was going on. This is downtown in the Peachtree area. What was he leading me too and why. I have my peace on me, so if he is up to some funny business Jason has taught me how to use my small 22 pistols. I had to laugh at myself. I went from Mary Magdalene to Madea in zero point zero seconds.

We walked up to a building and inside on the second floor was a suite. Inside was an office setting that had four other offices with window views of the city. It had a lounge with a kitchen. There were two sets of bathrooms, they had nice plush lounge areas. This was nice, and I'm curious to hear what he has planned for this space.

"Well, you have me here Matthew what is this place?"

"Jessica, I only signed up for a two-year contract with the firm you are employed with. If you can hear me out and don't interrupt me, please."

Just as he was saying that my phone rang. Who was that I thought so I let it go to voicemail? If it was Ms. Darlene, she would leave a message since she has Jayce. If it's anyone else, they can leave a message. Jason and I had already had our session over facetime.

"Matthew, okay I'm listening." Dang why is my phone going off like that.

I pulled it out and said it was Jason calling. I excused myself from Matthew to answer.

Hello, Hello I said with no response. He must have dialed me in error. Matthew began again.

He started to tell me how he was going to need more Marketing since he was going to start a new business. My phone rang, again.

"Hello this is Jessica can you hear me?" I continued to speak on my phone. This time it was silence, just dead air. Matthew motioned for me to turn on the speaker and he walked out the room.

"Hello Jason, are you there?" I could hear a commotion and nothing else. I heard some faint breathing. I spoke in a whisper; Jason are you in trouble please say something. That moment the other line went dead.

My heart started racing, I got Matthew to come in with me and I explained to him what was going on. He advised me that reception in those countries was not good. That nothing was wrong and to think positive regarding the situation. Just as he was finishing up the phone rang again, this time it was from an unknown number.

"Hello! I was angry.

"Jessica, I love you, let Jayce know that I love him too. If I don't make it back to the US, I know that you were my first love; everything I've done and worked for was to be a better man and provider for my family. I love you."

"Jason what's going on? Jason answered me. What is happening? I still had the phone on speaker. Matthew had gotten up to come over to me.

"Jessica, I love you". I heard in some whisper.

I heard some commotion and then some many shots, that I couldn't count anymore. The phone was going in and out with shots and movement. I was screaming into the phone Jason and hollering his name. The shots had stopped. I heard some language I couldn't make out, was It Spanish, French, or Creole. My heart was racing the commotion on the phone turned into a dial tone. I was frozen. I felt Matthew touching me. He pulled the phone out of my hand and placed it on the table and led me to the chair to sit down.

Once I got focused, Matthew was offering me a glass of water. I didn't want no Damn water my fiancé, my baby daddy was in trouble in Columbia. I screamed at Matthew I don't need any water I need a stiff drink. He looked at me and said I'll take you home Jessica. I felt him led me out to his car to drive me home. I spoke up Matthew, please don't take me home, until I hear something, I don't want to be alone.

"Jessica, would you like for me to take you to your parents?"

I snapped at him, I'm the black sheep of my family. The prodigal daughter, the one who got pregnant in college causing them to be ashamed of me. Heck no I snapped at him. Please just don't' leave me alone Matthew I'm asking you. I'm afraid and don't want to be left alone.

After riding in complete silence for almost forever. We pulled up to a gate that opened slowly. I was like dang, where are we. The garage opened and we pulled into this garage. Matthew led me into his home. It was beautifully decorated. He had items from all over the world. I asked to use the restroom and that strong drink.

When I got back out, I drank my drink and asked for another. I was talking to Matthew about what had just happened, giving my plans of leaving for Chicago in two days to meet Jason. I went over how he was going to set up a new office in Columbia and what could be going wrong.

My phone rang again. "Hello. Hello." I was getting very anxious. Matthew grabbed my phone and said, Hello. Jason hi are you there. We both were looking at the phone since we had it on speaker. Nothing was heard, some movement was there. "Hello, Jason I love you talk to me baby". I screamed into the phone. What was going on in my head? Bang, Bang, Pow, Pow.

I hollered out Nooooo OOOoooo Jason and dropped my phone. Matthew helped me off the floor and sat me on the sofa. I was crying and shaking he was holding onto me. After about an hour I finally stopped crying. Matthew made me a sandwich; I washed it down with a double of Royal crown apple.

Matthew had left the room and returned. He had some clothes in his hand. He led me to his guest room. It was late so I showered and changed into the clothes he gave me.

"Matthew, I really meant it when I said I didn't want to be alone. Can you lay with me until I fall asleep please?"

He laid down with me. I snuggled up to him and fell asleep.

I woke up to a vibrating sound. Looking around I was not sure of my surroundings. That vibrating was continuous. I had to find my phone. I eased out of Matthew arms to go find my phone. I had four missed calls with three voice messages, six text messages and one video message. Listening to the calls I began to cry hearing so much commotion in the background with minimum talking in French. I could hear a faint sound of pleas. Jason had left text messages of apologies and endearment of his love for me and Jayce. While watching the video message, I went numb seeing Jason's face and hearing him crying for help. Matthew took the phone from my hand. I cried in his arms as he held me.

My mind was going crazy, did I just see my entire future in a video go down the drain.

"Matthew, I apologize for being such a wreck, I don't mean to inconvenience you." I had tears still rolling down my face.

"Jessica, you are not alright?"

I grabbed on tight to Mathew kissing him, I wanted to escape those words I read and the visual of Jason from my mind. I continued to kiss Matthew until he gave him a kiss. He tried to resist me; I pulled him into me closer while grabbing onto his shorts.

"Jessica, you're not yourself right now, we can't do this."

"Matthew, I'm conscious of my actions please help me, ease my pain. I really need this now help me please I'm begging you." While kissing him deeper.

"Jessica, once we go....." she put her hands over my mouth while putting her hands over my manhood.

"Matthew don't deny me please I'm asking you to help me get through this?"

We continued kissing. I felt Matthew pull me closer while kissing me. He pulled me into the bedroom, lying me on the bed. He began to kiss me all over taking every inch of me into his mouth. Each inch of my body all over my nipples, easing down to my vagina. He took his tongue and danced all over my opening making me extremely wet. He placed his finger inside of me. I totally relaxed, closing my eyes, and enjoying him having his way with my body. Matthew used his tongue to comfort me dancing all over inside and outside of my clit. He pulled my hips up towards his mouth as I began to release myself. It was amazing.

He tried to stop. I pulled him closer to me. I could feel his hand on my thighs. He moved up closer and began to kiss all over my neck. I grabbed his manhood, oh my he was extremely large with a slight curve. I whispered make love to me Matthew. He began sliding the tip of his manhood up and down across my opening. Then he whispered relax, Jessica, then he pushed the tip inside of me and it wouldn't fit. I relaxed more and he began to move in and out until he was all the way inside of me. He was huge. I was moving with his every move while I felt every inch of him. We were at it for another twenty minutes until I felt him holding onto me extremely hard while his manhood felt like it was beginning to swell. He whispered cum with me Jessica, let it go baby. We released both at the same time. He rolled off me, gave me a kiss and held me until he drifted off to sleep.

THE CHURCH TRIED TO SHAME ME

You can Record Notes that can help you in your Flaws or Sins. Challenge Yourself

Chapter 12
Jason

I was glad to be filing out today to Columbia so this trip could be over, and I get back to marry my family. Jessica, Jayce, and I are going to be complete once we get married, they move to Chicago. I'd left instructions for my secretary to put down a deposit on an office that overlooked the river for her new marketing firm. I'd booked a showing for a nice home on the southside of town close to the city but far enough outside from major crime.

I fell off to sleep while in flight.

"Hey, St. John, wake up we are here."

We sat on our way in a private car to the location to see the building for the joint cartel. It went well and we met both assistants who would be working in the office. After all the formalities we signed off on the documents to proceed to our hotel.

I was ready to relax, first I went and purchased a few gifts for Jessica and Jayce. Getting ready to relax, Washington called my room to remind me of the meeting in a few hours with the potential new client. After hanging up from Washington I felt, something wasn't right in my spirit regarding this meeting. I dozed off to sleep.

Two hours later we were in the car going to the meeting spot. I told Washington that I thought we should leave something that felt strange to me. He gave me reassurance and then we walked into the building straight into an ambush. I immediately say from my side view three men dress in suits with their guns drawn. They had Mr. Gomez's nephew, who we met at the office tied up. He looked like he had been beaten bad.

"Hi Jose, what's going on? said Washington.

The second large guy near the door hit him in the head with his gun. I was left standing almost about to urinate on myself in fear.

"What are you doing here in Columbia, this is our city." Can you inform us who you work for?" this guy was speaking in Spanish to us. While Washington was drowsy, I answered in Spanish.

To the supervision of the men, I was fluent in Spanish also. I told them we were attorneys looking to start up a business in the country to assist the residents who are in the US.

At that moment Washington began to speak in an angered frenzy, he didn't realize I had the situation under control. He was fluent in Spanish, nor did he realize his money wasn't going to get us out of this mess.

I should have stuck with my gut. While we were still free, I dialed Jessica's number so I could at least speak with her. This was possibly my last moments of my life. I tried to get Washington to be quiet and let me speak since I was fluent in Spanish. The men had gone off to the side, I walked over to Jose and noticed he was barely alive. He glanced at me and said I should pray because we were all going to die. I immediately prayed that I live through this mess.

Washington was still in a frantic state. Shut up man I told him if he wanted to live to see his family again.

"I asked the gentleman, if we could be of service to them since we didn't come to do any harm to them."

They didn't respond, since I knew Spanish was over on the side whispering. To my surprise I hadn't noticed that Washington had made a call for reinforcement. The door burst open and an all-out shot out was happening. I ran for cover, praying that I could at least by myself some time.

I managed to call and speak with Jessica briefly. I told her I loved her, and I also apologize for messing up. During this time Washington was lit up with bullet holes and Jose was slumped over dead also. After another 30 minutes seemed like forever, I had been shot in my shoulder and in my side. I called, texted and left Jessica a video message.

I totally messed up. I prayed to God to protect and cover Jessica and Jayce as I took my last breath.

Chapter 13
Jessica

"Good Morning Ms. Darlene, how are you doing, how is my little man?"

"Jess, he is playing with those trucks, making all kinds of sounds. I'm enjoying him."

I didn't know how to tell her without tears flowing, but I know I needed to.

"Ms. Darlene, I think something has happened to Jason in Columbia." I went on to tell her all the details for as long as I could without breaking down crying.

"Jess, I'm on my way over, you don't' need to be alone."

"No, I'm not alone, I was at a business meeting when I got the call. Matthew is with me he also witness the call and say the video message from Jason."

"Jess, you don't worry about Jayce or your parents. I will tell them to you. Jessica, know that God has this in control and don't' worry yourself. I love you baby girl."

I broke down while saying goodbye. Matthew was right by my side. For the next two days, I couldn't get any answer on Jason's phone. I changed the plane ticket for Jayce to Matthew to accompany me to Chicago to get some answers. That moment my cell phone rang.

"May I speak with Jessica St. John?" Who could this be? I'm not St. John.

"You're speaking with Jessica." I answered.

It was the US Embassy in Colombia, to inform me that there had been an accident. They were sending Jason back to the US and wanted to know if I had a preference in where I wanted to have him sent.

Once I came to, Matthew explained that he went ahead and had Jason's body sent to Fulton Funeral Home. He stated that his firm had paid for all arrangements.

I couldn't believe that my life was going on this path, I needed to lie down.

Epilogue:
One Year Later

Hurry Jayce we are gonged to be left, your father going to leave us. I had to give myself that encouragement to get moving. I was moving extra slowly myself. Getting little people ready is extra work. We were on our way to visit Jason's grave and out to dinner. Yes, once I was able to get myself together, I flew out to Chicago and retrieved all of Jason's things. He has really had our lives planned. The surprise I received when I arrived. He picked us a nice, beautiful home; he was going to surprise me with my own office to do as I please. I know he wanted me to start my own Marketing Firm. During my time in Chicago, Matthew was by my side the entire time. We donated most of his things. The other items I shipped some to his parents and I kept some items for Jayce to have for his memories. He was young, but he was so wise for his age. I went and closed his accounts, to find out he had a safe deposit box also. Jason left me over three hundred dollars in his accounts, 2.3 million dollars spread out in two accounts, and a note to give his parents the brown envelope that was in the safe deposit box. He's left them 1 million dollars. His father was so happy they could afford a home in Haiti and Canada.

I only did a memorial service and split his ashes with his parents and myself. We received in the mail four days after the call from the embassy a package that Jason sent to us. It was delayed because the postal system in Columbia was slow. He picked out some wonderful souvenirs, I left them in the box because it was too painful. We didn't need any reminders that Columbia is where we lost our loved one.

"Jess, come on you're going to get left we have to go."

If you are wondering who is rushing me. Well, I must tell you after things started to settle back to a new normal. Matthew asked me to marry him, he was straight to the point. I didn't want to be a charity case, so I told him that he didn't' must feel obligated to marry me. He confused his love for me, from the time he first saw me up to the night that Jason was murdered. I tried to put things off if I could but four months later, I was losing weight and my hair was thinning out bad. Turned out what I thought was stress turned out to be Jasmine and Jessie, our twins. It was a shocker due to the timing when I slept with Mathew during my grief, and when Jason left for Columbia. Once the twins came, we did a DNA test. They are Matthew's, so that's what led me more to marry him.

From the night that Jason died the building surprise that I never got to hear about. Well both Matthew and Jason were thinking alike. I opened my own Marketing Firm, I named it. The J. St. John Jennings Consultant Firm.

Every Sunday we are at church with our family. You should never allow a mistake to cause you to feel shame. We all make mistakes, just take it one day at a time. The most hurting part of the shame is when it comes from your family, especially your church family.

Strive to achieve what God's plan is for you not what someone else's plans are for you.

"I knew you before I formed you in your mother's womb. Before you were born, I set you apart and appointed you as my prophet to the nations."
Jeremiah 1:5 NIV

You can follow me on Instagram @ielainejenkins_author

Thank You:
This was my second Christian Fiction book. As time goes by I will continue and get better at expressing my thoughts and give you a good applicable experience of both life and how to apply the scriptures.

Coming this Summer 2019

"" Disclaimer-—This Novel contains some Bad Language & Sexual Content—-"
Eugene "Gene" Royal Jr.

When Eugene, Jr accepts a position within the church. Will it be too late before she realizes that he Went and wasn't Sent by God. Will his actions show that the rumors of a PK are true of myths? This is the first book in the Series Royal Inheritance ~Pulpit Racketeering "The Royal Preachers Kids. Introducing Eugene Royal, Jr., Egypt Royal, Elijah Royal and Eve Royal the children of. Dr.

THE CHURCH TRIED TO SHAME ME

Eugene Royal Sr , Minister, and First Lady Essie Royal of the Just Jesus Cathedral of God from the novel (Sounds of Essence).

Eugene "Gene" Royal, Jr.

"So, Mr. Royal, today makes four months of these sessions. Do you feel you have made any progress in letting your father know that you are no longer wanting to be his associate minister? Would it be easier if you invited him to a session so you can inform him you're wanting to no longer be a part of the leadership?"

"Dr. Bennett, I've begun to make some comments towards me wanting to step down. It's that my father doesn't listen. He is wanting me to be him that he just doesn't see the reality of this. Every day he is comparing me to my brother, who is more than qualified for the position."

"Well, that information alone can help lead the conversation of getting out of the responsibility of being the associate minister. You could possibly suggest that he appoint your brother and you fall into a less out-front position at the church."

Here I am sitting in this counseling session trying to get my life back on track. It all started with me wanting to be noticed like my father. That has gotten me in trouble over the years and in this position I'm in now. It's terrible that your life is under a microscope most of the time. I'm the oldest man child of Dr. Reverend Eugene Royal, Sr. of the Just Jesus House Cathedral of God. and Mrs. Essie "Essence" Royal the soloist and founder of the Essence Soul Jazz Band. Yes, not only am I the eldest son but his name's sake, I'm Eugene "Gene" Royal, Jr. While growing up prior to this mess which I will explain later. My childhood was great and being the oldest I was exposed to so much. My mother was always with her band, either on tour or making albums along with servicing the church. While my father on the other hand was out servicing himself, that consisted of pride, lust, manipulator. My father, the preacher, wasn't always a man of God. Prior to him giving up his wicked ways or so we thought. The Reverend Dr. Eugene "Worm" Royal, Sr. Yes, my father the good ole Reverend used to be a slimy cold-blooded slick talker who could sell ice to an Eskimo. He could talk and persuade someone to do anything.

"Dr. Bennett, I have already thought of that. When I was almost about to speak with my father, he walked my brother telling us he is moving out of Houston. The things I'm dealing with now couldn't get any worse."

"Eugene, you have to take charge of this matter."

I knew that Dr. Bennett was right, this was not a good idea from the beginning. The saying be careful what you ask for, you just might get it. I would not be in this mess had my father's pride. The first time he mentioned having me be his assistant I should have just spoken up. Instead of saying NO, I encouraged this foolishness.

Just Jesus House of God / Church Meeting

"Thank you for joining us, Gene, you're late again so glad you could join us."

I could have reached over and choked Deacon Smith; he was always trying to bring attention to himself. Today was our weekly meeting before the midweek service and Sunday's worship service. The meeting would be a way to ease the news that I'm stepping down. It's just that my timing must be accurate.

"Good Evening." I spoke to everyone since I was put on the spot for being late. Today we were going to go over the upcoming Singles Conference. This year our church would be hosting the event. My father started his ministry work preaching at this conference. It is a permanent ministry we do every year. My father gave out the duties for the conference, and some other things that I wasn't listening to. My phone was vibrating, it wasn't going to stop so step out to check it. Excusing myself for a brief second I had six text messages and three voicemails from the same number one I didn't recognize.

I read and listened to all the messages. the fifth text message and listening to all the messages it was four messages that stood out. I smiled when I saw the messages from Abigail "Abby" as I called her immediately.

"Hi, Abby, I noticed your text and called me several times, is everything alright. I'm at the weekly church meeting."

"Gene, yes I'm fine. When you are finished with the meeting you can give me a call. It's not important I just miss talking to you this week. I told her I was in a meeting and would call her back shortly."

My timing was perfect, and the meeting was ending. Deacon Smith was preparing to pray so we could adjourn. I sat and chopped it up with a few of the members and left.

Abigail "Abby" Bless

Thank you everyone for allowing me to speak to you today. In the last two years we have been following the performance of local bands throughout the city. To make our organization one of the best in marketing we must know who and what groups we will be promoting. The upcoming Soul Jazz Fest will be approaching real soon. If you would pull out your packets you will see the main two bands that we have contracted our firm. In your packet you will see the request made of the clients and the requirements of our firm. There will be two groups and each group is already assigned to a team as well as it's team members. I want to thank you in advance, and we will meet again in one week to finalize. Does anyone have any questions?

"Ms. Simmons, is it okay if I can speak with you after the meeting please."

"Yes, Monica, that will be fine." She wanted to know if it would be a conflict of interest if she was assisting on the advertisement for the band, since she was a backup singer. I had to assure her that her personal life doesn't and shouldn't interfere with her professional career.

Today was a long day. I had the worst morning and now I'm starting to feel almost as bad as I did this morning. I woke up with a bad headache after taking a few Excedrin I made it to the office late, but I made it. This good job pays the bills and supplies me with good resources throughout the city.

I'm Abigail Bless Simmons, my parents, siblings, and I moved to Houston from Seattle, WA almost five years ago. I was fresh out of college from Prairie View, with a degree in Business Management.

The first thoughts of relocating were bad, but it's turned out to be great. I have a new graduate. It was easier for me to secure a job immediately with a Marketing Firm in Houston as COO of Advertising.

Making way to my car only to be hit with a sharp pain in my head. Early I had taken a few Excedrin, but this pain was getting the best of me. I commanded my car to call Gene which I was sent to voicemail. Using voice command for text messages to him and then I left a message.

I've been seeing a very nice young man for over a year now. Gene Royal, son of Dr. Eugene Royal Sr., Gene is an assistant minister at one of Houston's mini mega churches. We met at a function my job showcased for the community. I met his entire family and one of my sorority sisters is his sister-in-law.

Finally, the medicine began to work, and I left the parking lot headed home.

Once I got home, I took a lavender and coconut milk bath. This was one of my favorite ways to relax. I'm excited to see what our team is going to come up with. The first experience I had with the firm was a large BBQ competition and the local competitors wanted the best advertisement for the event and their businesses. The rush that I received during that event was phenomenal, we had billboards, TV ads, radio commercials to promote the event. My thoughts were broken with the ringing of my phone.

"Hi, Beautiful how are you?" hearing Gene's voice was that extra I needed for a relaxing night.

"Hey, baby I'm doing better now that I'm able to hear your voice. I had a rough start; I woke up with a terrible headache that lingered until an hour ago."

"I'm sorry to hear that sweetheart. Hopefully you are feeling better."

We talked for almost an hour until just catching up, we tried to make plans, but our schedules just are too busy. He said a brief prayer and we said our good nights.

WAKING UP
to the WRONG
Woman
INGRID SYMONE &
MURDA (RVC)

Chapter 1

Mount Airy Lodge, PA

"Do y'all see her?" Caleb nodded in the woman's direction.

Both Jeff and Shamar, his friends looked in the direction which Caleb nodded his head. It was like the scene out of Friday when Ice Cube and Chris Tucker was looking at Ms. Parker, when they both yelled. "DAMMMNNNNN!!"

"She bad as hell," Jeff said admiring the woman's beauty. "She is bad as hell," Shamar had to admit.

"She got some bad friends too," Shamar said noticing the other two girls she was with.

"Yeah, they cool but baby girl one of a kind," Caleb was stuck on the woman who had just took a seat at the table with her assume to be friends.

On the opposite side of the room.

Aaliyah sat with her sorority sisters. Vicky and Keyana. Vicky and Key were having a wonderful time but for some reason Liyah wasn't having as much fun. Truth be told Liyah was tired of meeting every month for the girl's night or trips. Her head hung low as she scrolled through her Facebook page. Liyah was in the need of a male companion. She wa a successful writer, good looks and extraordinary ambitions and she needed a man in her life to make her complete. When she looked up from her iPhone it was like GOD had answered her prayers, because he was sitting across the room with two to other guys. He looked to be tall from what she could see. He had a freshly shaved bald head and full shadowed beard his muscular frame made her panties moist from just looking at him. While Liyah lusted over Caleb from across the room, he never noticed her, because he was busy watching the mysteriously beautiful woman, he couldn't keep his eyes off.

"Fuck this I got to say something to her," he said getting up from the bar walking in the direction of the woman's table. As he closed the distance between them one of the other girls that was with the mysterious woman got up from the table rushing away covering her mouth with her hand. From the looks of it she had to throw up. As she ran away so did his chances of confronting the beautiful woman, seeing her chase after her beautiful friend in a hurry.

Caleb got to the table just as the last woman was getting up. She had just paid the bill and was gathering her and her girlfriends' things they had left behind. While pushing away from the table.

"Excuse me miss." Caleb spoke in his deep baritone voice, catching the woman's attention causing her to look up from the table.

At first Monique was bothered by the disturbance but when she looked up and noticed how attractive Caleb was, she was at a loss to words.

"How, how may I love you; I mean help you?" Monique asked she was quite embarrassed she covered her mouth with her hand. 'I'm sorry, she apologized.

Caleb smiled showing off his perfect pearly whites, "No I'm sorry for interrupting you, I was wondering about your homegirl who got up and ran from the table."

"Oh," Monique was disappointed her expression changed. Caleb could tell and apologized again with his eyes.

"Which one?" she asked.

"The light brown skin one she was kind of thick with the nice lips." He said just in a whisper seeing how sensitive the young lady was.

Monique could tell the way Caleb's eyes lit up when he described Kabria that he really liked what he saw.

"Oh, you are talking about Bria," she said.

"Is that her name?" he asked, "Do she have a man?"

"Why don't' you give me your number and you can ask her yourself." She stated.

"I'm asking to many questions, Huh?" Caleb asked.

"I just don't want to speak for her feel me?"

"I get it," Caleb said as he looked through his wallet for his card. When he found one, he handed it over to her.

It Read:

Caleb Champion,

Best-selling Author screen play writer

917-757-3777 O:917-757-3555 C:917-777-37785 F

"Okay Mr. Champion I'll be sure I give this to Bria," Monique said as she smiled and walked away.

On the opposite side of the bar....

Liyah watched as Caleb gave Monique his card, she didn't even know him, but she was in her feelings she was jealous as Monique exited the Bar Liyah burned holes in her back with her eyes.

Vicky noticed Liyah staring in Caleb's direction and put her on blast, "You gone keep, looking or you gone go one there and shoot your shot."

Liyah tried to play it off "girl what you are talking about?"

"Don't play dumb with me I see you looking at that fine ass chocolate specimen of a man."

"What?" you are bugging.

"If you scared, we'll come with you because he does get some fine ass friends, "Key added her two cents.

"Come on" Vicky said pulling Liyah by her arm up off the bar stool in the direction of Caleb and his crew.

"Stooop" Liyah put resistance as they tugged on her.

"Stop acting like that, you know you want to go Vicky pulled on her arm.

"Ok Ok Ok let me fix myself Liyah said stopping to make sure her clothes were intact.

At the bar Caleb sat back down with his boys

"So, what happen?" Jeff asked.

"Man, by the time I got over there she was gone, but I gave her friend my number. I hope she calls Caleb sound so defeated.

"Oh, shit check it out Shamar directed, their attention to Liyah and her girls approaching the rapidly before Caleb could respond the girls were at hit a bar on the side of him and his crew.

"What's up, Fellas, my name is Vicky these are my girls Keyana and Liyah."

All the girls spoke but Liyah was a little shy. The other girls had chosen. Vicky was hollering at Jeff and Keyana was smiling in Shamar's face so that left. Caleb and Liyah Caleb's mind was till on Kabria. But when he started to pay attention to Liyah, she was a beauty too. She favored Lorie Harvey but with green eyes, she was opposite of Kabria, whereas Kabria was on the shorter side with the brown skin, thick thighs, and ass. Liyah stood about five foot eight inches red bone. She was slim but dam she had a fat ass on her too. I guess you could describe her as being slim, thick.

Caleb's mood started to change immediate once he noticed how beautiful Liyah was too.

"Why you actin all shy have a seat," Caleb pulled the bar stool out for her.

"If I have a seat that girl, you gave your number too ain't gone wanna fight me, is she?" Liyah asked while rolling her eyes at him.

"Oh, you saw that huh?" he asked.

"Yes, I did and truthfully I'm kinda jealous," she playfully admitted.

"No, you do not stop playing he leaned to get a little closer to her.

"Hold up what you are doing?" she asked as she moved slightly away. She was playing but truthfully, she wanted him all over her, but she didn't want to seem too easy.

"He leaned close to her and sniffed her neck, "I'm trying to make sure you don't' stink."

"What boy stop playing with me, I look like I stink?' she asked with a bit of attitude.

"I don't know. You and your girls been tearing up that dance floor up all night," he continued to joke.

She had enough of his jokes, she balled up her tiny fist and punch him lightly in his chest. When her fist landed on his chest, his chest was nice and hard. She could tell he worked out. She liked what she felt and was extremely impressed.

"Owwww," he grabbed his chest like she had hurt him with her soft punch.

"I see you like to play a lot what are you a comedian?" she asked.

"NO actually, I'm a writer, I'm into movie production and books plays things like that." He responded.

"Stop playing I see you like joking." She replied.

"What makes you think I'm joking?" Caleb asked talking a sip of his drink.

"Because I don't' know how you know but I'm a writer, and I'm working on a play right now, titled Lock Down Love.

"WOW, that's dope I'm not joking though." He slid her his business card. She took the card and read it.

"WOW, she was amazed she couldn't believe it he was her match. He was tall, handsome, nice teeth and they shared the same occupation. For her it was love at first sight, now she was even more attracted to him.

"So where are you from?" he asked.

"I'm from St. Albans, Queens" she stated.

"Damn," that's crazy I'm from New York to I'm from Brooklyn Marcy Projects. To be exact. Growing up in the saint Albans I see you a good girl huh?'

"Well, you know what they say Good Girls like Bad Boys?"

"And what makes you think I'm a Bad Boy?"

"Growing up in Marcy projects, I assume you've been around somethings."

"True that doesn't mean I'm a bad boy. That couldn't be farthest from the truth. I've worked extremely hard not to be stereotyped like the average young Black man growing up in the projects." He stated. "I won't say that I wasn't exposed nor am I blind to what happens growing up in that environment.

"Well, I'm sorry that I offended you." Liyah said.

"No need to apologize it's all good. Like I said I worked hard to become the man I am. You are right I've seen a lot as I stated. When I was young my parents both worked hard to keep me out of trouble, because my older brother was nothing but trouble. So, they both worked hard to move us out of the hood. My mother was a nurse while my father drove the local transit bus; and did anything else he could do to get money to move us out of the hood.

When I was about nine, we moved out of Marcy and my parents brought a house in Williamsburg. Everything was good until one night my father was working his side job at the gas station and a group of young boys came in to rob the spot.

Liyah could tell as he told his story he was getting emotional.

"You don't have – ", he cut her off.

"No, it's ok. Then he continued." So, they came in to rob the spot. My dad gave them everything they asked for and they still killed him. After that thing got extremely hard for my mom. She couldn't keep up with the payment on the house and boom were back in the projects.

Caleb was blinking back some tears that he did not realize until one slowly fell from his eye. He didn't mind at that point since he was in tone with his emotions. His mother taught him to always be true to his feelings no matter what.

"So now I've told my story what's yours?"

Liyah didn't want to go into her life story after hearing Caleb's story full of hardship, but Caleb kept pressing so she gave a glimpse of her life.

"Well, both of my parents are still a live my mom is a retired pharmacist, and my dad is retired military sergeant. He's the number one man in my life."

"Oh, I see you're a daddy's girl." Caleb teased.

"You better know it, He spoiled me my whole life, that's why I stopped you. When you told me about your father dying. I wouldn't know what to do without my dad. He's the best man in the world, me and my family are so lucky to have a man like him. "

"I see I have a tough act to follow," Caleb said while grabbing her hand landing a kiss on it. Liyah almost melted his lips felt so good "Damn" she thought to herself.

"Well, if you plan on being around you certainly have some big shoes to fill." She smiled.

"I think I can manage that, "Caleb replied full of confidence.

"I'm warning you I'm a bit much." Liyah replied.

Liyah knew she was pushing it knowing how she wasn't as much into doing some of the things that was on the agenda for the trip planned for the weekend. Her girls knew it too, but in Liyah mind she wanted Caleb and had to prove a point to herself.

Let's see how this all plays out for her.

"I'm up for the challenge." He winked at her.

His overconfident swagger turned her on. This man was perfect for her. The rest of the night went by smooth Aaliyah's girls and Caleb crew hit it off big. It was like everything about his man turned her on. They headed back to Caleb's cabin where they kicked it all night Liyah and Caleb's filled in the blanks on the rest of their interest and dislikes. Everything went well. It was during their conversation. Aaliyah lied a bit. It wasn't anything major, but she pretended to have a little more in common than they really did.

Caleb admitted he was somewhat of an extrovert and that's where the lie came in. Liyah functioned as if she was into the things Caleb was, but truth be told she wasn't more of the conservative type. Being with Liyah and her friends took Caleb's' mind off Kabria. Caleb sat back and thought for a moment after everything settled down. "Damn this girl is perfect for me, I may have found the woman I've been looking for."

Chapter 2

The next morning the sun rose, its rays shinned bright through Kabria cabin window.

This trip was what she truly needed at this point in her life, although her girls did these trips often this one was important. It was what she called getting back to herself. Over the last year her life changed as she knew it. With her loving mother, bff and home girls the worse thing was being in a relationship with a man who she thought was the one. It went from I'm his everything to pure hate he felt towards her. Myron became abusive emotionally, verbally, and to physical. IT's been almost six months since Kabria packed up all her belongings one afternoon and didn't look back.

Myron really showed himself at one of her recognition conferences. Kabria was recognized for being a ghostwriter for a new upcoming author; although it was confidential the author wanted to recognize her. When Myron arrived late of course he was extremely jealous of Kabria's fame. IT was some real movers and shakers at the event. Today his words still ring in her head at times. He spit them with venom, towards her, "You not Zane or Sista Souljah that little book wont' go far. These people are just pumping your little head up." Everyone was looking at Kabria, when her newest friend in the industry Jay Phoenix came over to pull Myron to the side.

Kabria was good for the remainder of the event whatever Jay said to him he was like a kid in church. Respectful, smiled and held onto her like she was the prize trophy that night. It was all an act; he was a fool even worse after that.

Kabria saved up her money from those little ghostwriting gigs, since it' paid her from fifteen hundred to five thousand dollars a novel. She packed her stuff one day and didn't look back. Brought her a nice little compartment as her best friend called it, an apartment slash condominium for fifty thousand a cute end unit in the suburbs with a nice sky view.

Back to the current setting...

Kabria, Monique, and Cindy had fallen asleep late last night. While watching old reruns of Good Times. Today was going to be an action-packed day for her girls. After hey ate breakfast, they we going to hit the slopes and after that they were going to the bungee jumping site. Kabria loved doing the outdoor things. She could watch a whole football game in the stands while it snowed. Kabria wasn't your average chick; she was a child a beautiful one at that who enjoyed everything life had to offer. From sports to most outdoor activities. She lived life to the fullest had fun doing it, she could be called the life of the party.

Kabria was in the bathroom getting ready for their date as she sang along to the music that played from her iPhone. She fixed her long black hair in a ponytail. Yes, it was all her natural hair. As she looked in the mirror, she admired her own beauty. "Yes, girl you are the shit" she said. To herself as she grabbed her phone off the sink; she opened the bathroom door. Monique overheard her talking to herself and butted in.

"Girl, you need to stop with your conceited ass, Monique said as she brushed pass Kabria to get into the bathroom.

Kabria ignored her friend; she knew MoMo was struggling herself with self-love. So, she just let her have that comment, while replying to her.

"I can't help it if I look good," Kabria's confidence was always on a million.

"Well, you ain't the only one" Monique's said as she blew a kiss in Kabria direction. Monique was right all three of the girls were beauties. Monique and Kabria shared the same features of medium brown skin, thick thighs, curvy hips, and perfectly shaped breast. Cindy was a light olive-green complexion that she inherited from her father side of the family, African Italian, with her Cuban mother's beautiful thick body to add. Cindy's long black hair was all natural like Monique and Kabria's. Cindy was the tallest of the three, as she was also much thicker. Any man would love to have any one of these smart beautiful girls.

Monique picked up where Bria had left off singing in the bathroom as she sang along to Boss Chick, by Rasheeda. MoMo, fumbled through her pocketbook looking for her lip liner. She stumbled across the business card Caleb had given her yesterday while she was rushing out the bar.

"Oh Shit Briaaaaaaaa!!!," Monique called from the bathroom. A few seconds later Bria busted into the bathroom.

"What do your aggravating ass want."" Bria asked with her hand on her hip.

"I forgot to give you this," Monique handed Bria the business card. Bria took it and looked at it.

"What's this?"

"After you and Cindy ran out the bar yesterday this fine ass dude came up to me and said he'd been watching you from across the bar. He started asking me questions about you. so, I told him to give me his number and I would give it to you. so here you go. "

"What, I'm not calling no creep that was watching me from across the bar."

"You so stuck up," Monique huffed. "Dude didn't look like he was a creep. He was fine as hell and form the looks of it he had a lil change too.

"Girl shut your gold-digging ass up." Kabria shouted, "How do you know he got money?"

Monique was very observant; she picked that trait up from her father who was a con artist. He taught her how to people watch, however she barley used that learned trait when it really counted.

"He had a nice as Rollie on," Monique rolled her eyes at Kabria.

"Girl Bye! I'm not calling no nigga who was stalking me from a across the bar." She left Monique standing in bathroom.

"Well, if you don't want him, I'll take him," Monique shouted towards Bria from the bathroom.

"GO AHEAD HOE!!!," Kabria yelled back.

One thing about the three girls they loved each other, and they knew of the code that was unspoken. Although Monique said I'll take him, and Bria's reply was gone ahead they both knew it wasn't reality. They never crossed each other always looking out for one another.

The same morning on the other side of the building.

Aliya and her girls were just getting up after getting in from hanging with Caleb and his crew until the wee hours in the morning Aaliyah was awake, but she was just lying in the bed looking up at the ceiling daydreaming. The night with Caleb; had been beautiful and he was a perfect gentleman. He didn't try to make any sexual advance towards her although the vibe was there. She wanted him so bad, but she didn't 'want him to think she was some fast ass thot who only wanted a weekend fling. She wanted more than that, she wanted him to respect her and consider her to be his girl sometime soon.

She was laying there thinking what sex with Caleb would be like. Those thoughts made her close her eyes and slide her hand down her Victoria secret panties. She touched her vagina in away only she could. She imagined it was Caleb's tongue flicking back and forth over her clit. The thought and feeling drove her crazy. As she kept playing with herself. She thought back to when she had felt Caleb chest in the bar. She started to moan lightly as she played with herself. she caressed her breast with her free hand. Her moans grew louder the closer she came to climax "Oh oh oh don't stop baby don't stop."

She was so into it she was talking to Caleb, and he wasn't even there. "I'm cumming!!!!" she bit down on her bottom lip to keep from screaming as she squirted all over the bed soaking the sheet.

"Damn," she said trying to catch her breath. Aaliyah was no stranger to pleasing herself she had been without a man for quite some time now she wasn't into causal sex so masturbation was her only option. She hadn't had sex in so long she felt like a virgin.

"Knock, Knock, Knock., three knocks on the bedroom door caused her to jump a little. "Who is it?" she asked aggressive she was upset someone ruined her moment.

"It's me," Vicky said opening the door walking in uninvited.

"What do you want?" change huffed.

"I came to see if you gone hit the slopes with me and Keyana with your nasty ass," Vicky said letting her know she heard her.

Liyah covered her mouth with her hand embarrassed.

"Don't get all embarrassed now miss goody two shoes with ya freak ass." I knew you was some undercover freak shit." Vicky teased her.

"Shut up and get out." Liyah threw a pillow at her.

"Are you coming with us or not?"

"Did Keyana hear me too?"

"Hell, no wit her hoe ass, Caleb's friend Shamar came over like an hour after we got in. She been in there getting her back blown out all morning."

"You are lying," Liyah said.

"Girl, you know how she is with her fast ass, are you coming or what? "

"Vic you know I'm not really into all that skiing and all that bungee jumping shit."

Vic gave her the side eye. "That ain't what you told Caleb last night, I heard your lying ass," Vicky said.

"That's different I will jump off the empire state building for that nigga."

"You are so stupid," Vicky laughed as she left out of the room and closed the door behind her, while saying get your nasty self in the shower.

Liyah got up taking the soaked sheets off the bed from her sexcapade. After she got them changed, she showered to get ready for the day. She took a long hot shower still thinking about the man of her dreams. *"What is he gone think when he finds out I lied about liking all the things he does."* Shit it is what it is we will cross that bridge when we get there. But for now, I got to do what I got to do get my man."

Chapter 3

Caleb, Jeff, and Shamar stood at the bottom of the slop waiting on the ski lift to take them to the top of the slope. As they waited Shamar told them how he sexed Keyana all morning.

"Bro she is a freak. I'm telling you she did somethings to me I thought only porn stars got paid to do."

"You are lying Nigga!" you always blowing some shit up. Jeff said they got on the ski lift. While they were going up Caleb noticed Bria preparing herself to go down the slope. "There she goes right there." Caleb pointed "DAMN Ain't no way we are going make it up there before she goes down." And right he was she pulled her goggles down and took flight down the slope. Caleb watched as Kabria glide down the slope like a pro. When they got to the top of the slope Caleb rushed to get to the front so he could be first down the slope at a rapid pace. He got to the bottom and again disappointed. Kabria was nowhere in sight. Caleb waited for Jeff and Shamar at the bottom of the slope while he looked around desperately in search of Kabria.

As Kabria, MoMo, and Cindy walked back to the Lodge laughing and joking Cindy started throwing her guts up again.

"Girl, what the hell is your problem why you keep throwing up?" Bria asked genuinely concerned. People walked by looking some out of concern others just being nosey.

"I'm ok, I'm ok, Let's go Cindy said wiping her mouth then taking a sip of water.

"If you say so," Bria was not willing to go back and forth with her at this point. Bria knew that she was hiding something it was only a matter of time before she would have to tell them what was going on.

Cindy really wasn't' feeling well at this so they decided to head back to the cabin. When they made it back to the cabin, they ordered some food and put on Netflix to watch a new series called A Game for Fools. It was supposed to be a hit from what was being talked about on social media. The food came and they didn't waste any time digging in.

"Girl y'all need to try these," MoMo said pushing her container of bison nachos forward Cindy took some followed by Kabria. Kabria put nachos in her mouth and immediately spit it out.

"What the Hell," is this Bria asked taking a sip of her water.

"Bison Nachos," MoMo answered stuffing her face.

"Bison? Bitch you on some white people shit, Black people don't eat that shit.

MoMo couldn't do anything but laugh Bria was crazy. MoMo looked over to Cindy for her approval, but she was headed towards the bathroom to spit her guts again.

Seconds later Cindy was in the bathroom bent over the toilet throwing her guts up for umpteenth time and now MoMo and Kabria were starting to get worried.

"Cindy what's going on?" Bria asked standing in the doorway of the bathroom. Cindy stuck her finger up as to say wait a minute while she continued to hurl. When she finished, she brushed her teeth then she joined MoMo and Bria on the couch. When she sat down, she immediate began to cry."

"What's wrong? MoMo asked concerted about her girl.

It's a long story Cindy admitted through sniffles.

"Shit, we ain't got nothing but time and we ain't going nowhere until you spill it. Now get to talking. Bria was on her. She wanted answers and she wanted them now. The three of them were like sisters and they didn't keep secrets from each other. So, she wanted to know what was going on.

"Well, y'all remember when we took that trip to Miami?" Cindy asked yeah, we remember." both MoMo and Bria answered at the same time.

"Well, when I went to get the rental, I met this handsome guy from Philly. We started kicking it and one night while you all were asleep, I slid out and went to his room. The next thing you know we were having sex and now I think I'm pregnant," she started to cry as she ended the story.

"Oh, don't cry," Bria said while comforting her pulling her close to her side.

"How could you be so irresponsible and not use protection Cindy." Bria was asking. "Was the dick good?"

"Please Bria don't be mad at me." Cindy sniffled.

"So, what about ole dude?" MoMo asked.

"He doesn't know. I haven't seen or spoke to him since that night." Cindy said with her head held down ashamed. she could feel her tears began to flow even heavier.

"Wow, Bitch you are a straight up sneaky a hoe" Bria said, causing MoMo to laugh and that caused Cindy to cry harder.

"Oh no don't be doing all that crying now, don't cry, you know we got you no matter what you still our girl." Bria said. Inside Bria was glad it wasn't that crazy dude Cindy was with prior. Omg that hot girl summer, back to the street's booty done got my girl knock the fuck up. Bria laughed to herself.

"But what we bout to do is I'm gonna shoot down to the gift shop and see if they got a pregnancy test down there and we gonna make sure you pregnant or not. Bria said grabbing her jacket and headed out the door.

You can follow me on Instagram
@ielainejenkins_author

My other books are at
WEBSITE: www.elainesbookpalace.com
Soulful Sounds of Essie
Beauty Butter Bread
Cuffed by a Chauffer
Mansions and Money
The Journey of Love

Don't miss out!

Visit the website below and you can sign up to receive emails whenever Elaine Jenkins publishes a new book. There's no charge and no obligation.

https://books2read.com/r/B-A-GTVV-CVZFC

BOOKS2READ

Connecting independent readers to independent writers.

www.ingramcontent.com/pod-product-compliance
Lightning Source LLC
Chambersburg PA
CBHW052219150726
48002CB00003B/1188